For all the hardworking
mama bears and their cubs

BEACH LANE BOOKS · An imprint of Simon & Schuster Children's Publishing Division · 1230 Avenue of the Americas, New York, New York 10020 · Copyright © 2021 by Kimberly Gee · All rights reserved, including the right of reproduction in whole or in part in any form. · BEACH LANE BOOKS is a trademark of Simon & Schuster, Inc. · For information about special discounts for bulk purchases, please contact Simon & Schuster Special Sales at 1-866-506-1949 or business@simonandschuster.com. · The Simon & Schuster Speakers Bureau can bring authors to your live event. For more information or to book an event, contact the Simon & Schuster Speakers Bureau at 1-866-248-3049 or visit our website at www.simonspeakers.com. · Book design by Karyn Lee · The text for this book was set in Supernett. · The illustrations for this book were rendered in black Prismacolor and colored digitally. · Manufactured in China · 1120 SCP · First Edition · 10 9 8 7 6 5 4 3 2 1 · Library of Congress Cataloging-in-Publication Data · Names: Gee, Kimberly, author, illustrator. · Title: Sad, sad bear! / Kimberly Gee. · Description: First edition. | New York : Beach Lane Books, [2021] | Audience: Ages 3–8. | Audience: Grades 2–3. | Summary: Bear is very sad when Mommy must go to work and leave him at Cub Care, but his first day turns out to be a good one. · Identifiers: LCCN 2020029769 (print) | ISBN 9781534452718 (hardcover) | ISBN 9781534452725 (eBook) · Subjects: CYAC: Sadness—Fiction. | Day care centers—Fiction. | Bears—Fiction. · Classification: LCC PZ7.G2577 Sad 2021 (print) | DDC [E]—dc23 · LC record available at https://lccn.loc.gov/2020029769

Sad, Sad Bear

Kimberly Gee

Beach Lane Books
New York London Toronto Sydney New Delhi

Bear is sad.

Mommy is going to work.

Bear is going to Cub Care.

And he does not know anyone there at all.

This makes Bear very . . .

very . . .

But then Bear makes a friend.

And another friend.

And another friend!

Bear and his new friends build.

And cook.

And take a little hike.

They have a picnic.

And sing the clean-up song.

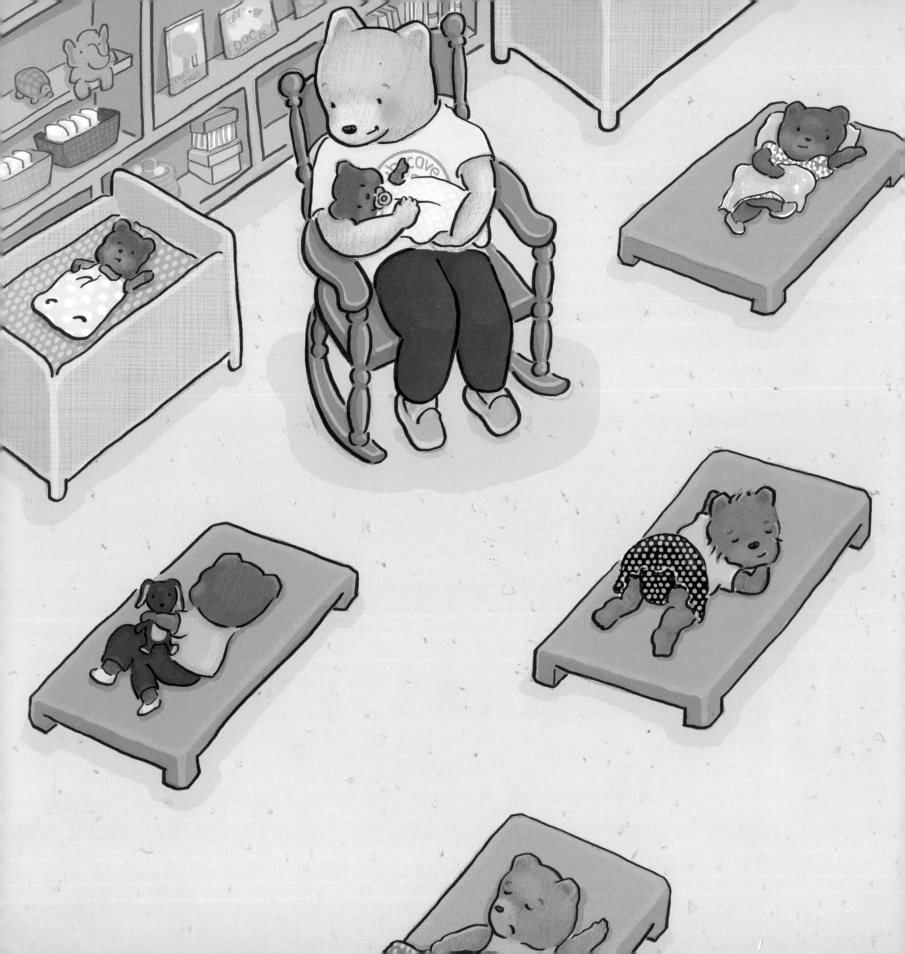

Then it is quiet time.

When Bear wakes up, Mommy is back!

Bear tells her all about his day.

And says goodbye to his new friends.

He cannot wait
to come back
again tomorrow.